Sherlock Holmes and The Cat Burglar

Mabel Swift

Copyright © 2024 by Mabel Swift

All rights reserved. No part of this publication may be reproduced in any form, electronically or mechanically without permission from the author.

This is a work of fiction and any resemblance to any person living or dead is purely coincidental.

Contents

Chapter 1	1
Chapter 2	8
Chapter 3	13
Chapter 4	20
Chapter 5	26
Chapter 6	33
Chapter 7	41
Chapter 8	44
Chapter 9	50
Chapter 10	54
Chapter 11	60
Chapter 12	65
Chapter 13	72
A note from the author	76

Chapter 1

The sweltering heat of the London summer bore down upon the city, seeping through the open windows of 221B Baker Street. Inside, Holmes paced restlessly across the sitting room, looking this way and that as if searching for a mystery hidden within the familiar surroundings. Dr Watson, seated in his favourite armchair, observed his friend's agitation with a mixture of amusement and concern.

"My dear Watson," Holmes declared, pausing mid-stride, "it has been precisely seventeen days since our last case. Seventeen days of intellectual stagnation!" He tapped his fingers against his thigh in a staccato rhythm, a habit Watson had come to associate with his friend's growing impatience.

Watson set aside the newspaper he had been perusing and said, "Come now, Holmes. You know as well as I do that these lulls are but temporary. A new mystery will present itself soon enough."

Holmes turned to face his companion, his angular features etched with frustration. "But when, Watson? When? London teems with secrets and crimes, yet here we sit, idle as schoolboys on holiday."

"Perhaps," Watson suggested gently, "you might consider this a well-deserved respite. After all, our last case was particularly taxing."

Holmes waved away the notion with a dismissive flick of his wrist. "Respite? Bah! You know me, my mind rebels at stagnation."

With a sigh, Holmes strode to the window, his tall figure silhouetted against the bright summer light. He stood there, hands clasped behind his back, eyes narrowed as he surveyed the bustling street below.

Watson returned to his perusal of the day's news.

"Look there, Watson," Holmes said suddenly. "Do you see that young woman hurrying past? Notice how she clutches her reticule, her knuckles white with tension. She glances over her shoulder every few steps, clearly fearful of pursuit."

Watson put down his newspaper again and joined his friend at the window, peering down at the figure Holmes had singled out. "Perhaps she's simply in a hurry," he suggested.

Holmes shook his head. "No, no. Observe the way she walks. Short, quick steps, but lacking the purposeful stride of someone with a destination in mind. She's fleeing, Watson, but from what or whom, I cannot say."

As Watson watched, he had to admit that the woman did seem distressed.

Holmes continued his observations, his words coming faster now as his mind raced ahead.

"And there, that gentleman with the red carnation in his buttonhole. See how he fidgets with his watch chain? He's clearly nervous, and he's perspiring far more than this heat alone would account for. He's waiting for someone, Watson, someone he fears may not arrive."

Watson nodded, fascinated as always by his friend's ability to read the minutiae of human behaviour. "What do you suppose has him so anxious?" he asked.

"It could be any number of things," Holmes mused. "A clandestine meeting, perhaps. Or maybe he's about to engage in some illicit transaction. Whatever the case, he's clearly out of his depth."

As they continued to observe the ebb and flow of humanity on Baker Street, Holmes pointed out more individuals who caught his discerning eye. There was an elderly gentleman whose limp seemed to vary in severity depending on who was nearby, suggesting a ruse rather than a genuine ailment. A pair of women, ostensibly strangers, exchanged a furtive glance and a subtle hand signal as they passed each other, hinting at some secret society or clandestine organisation.

"You see, Watson?" Holmes said, his earlier restlessness now replaced by enthusiasm. "London is awash with mysteries, each person on that street a walking enigma. Surely among them, there must be someone in desperate need of our services."

Watson said, "I have no doubt that you're right. But remember, not every curious behaviour indicates a crime or a case worthy of your talents. Sometimes, people are simply people, with all their quirks and eccentricities."

Holmes turned from the window. "Perhaps you're right, my dear fellow. But can you blame me for hoping? For yearning to sink my teeth into a truly perplexing problem?"

"Not at all," Watson replied with a warm smile. "Your mind craves stimulation, as it always has. I merely suggest patience. Our next great adventure will find us soon enough, I'm certain of it."

With that, Holmes returned to his chair, fingers steepled beneath his chin as he lost himself in thought. Watson, knowing his friend's moods all too well, settled back with his newspaper, ready to wait out the lull until the next great mystery presented itself.

The quiet of 221B Baker Street was suddenly broken by a sharp rap at the front door. Watson started at the sound. He began to rise from his comfortable armchair, his joints creaking slightly as he did so.

"I'll get it," he said. "Mrs Hudson is out for the morning. It's probably just—"

But before Watson could finish his sentence, Holmes had already leapt from his chair with the agility of a much younger man.

"No, no, Watson," Holmes called over his shoulder as he bounded towards the door. "I'll attend to it. It could be a potential client!"

Watson settled back into his chair, a bemused smile on his face as he listened to the rapid footfalls of his friend descending the stairs. The muffled sound of the front door opening reached his ears, followed by the low murmur of voices. Try as he might, Watson couldn't make out the words being exchanged, but he found himself leaning forward in his seat, straining to hear any clue that might indicate the nature of their visitor.

After a few moments, the door closed with a soft thud, and Watson heard Holmes' footsteps on the stairs once more. This time, however, they lacked the eager spring of before. When Holmes re-entered the sitting room, the excitement had drained from his face, replaced by a look of profound disappointment.

"Well?" Watson prompted, eyebrows raised in question.

Holmes sighed heavily, slumping back into his chair. "Nothing of consequence, I'm afraid," he said. "Merely an elderly woman looking for her lost cat and asking if I'd seen him."

"Ah, I see. Poor thing must be worried about her pet."

"Indeed," Holmes replied, though his tone suggested he was far more concerned with his own disappointment than the plight of the missing feline.

A thought struck Watson. "I say, perhaps we should offer to look for the cat. It might not be the most thrilling case, but it would give you something to do, at least."

Holmes fixed Watson with a look of mild incredulity. "My dear Watson, while I appreciate your attempt to alleviate my boredom, I must remind you that we are not in the business of searching for missing cats, dogs, or any other manner of household pets. Our talents are better suited to more substantial matters."

Watson nodded, conceding the point. "Yes, of course. You're quite right. I do hope she finds her cat, though."

Holmes settled deeper into his chair. "I hereby declare that I shall not move from this very spot until a client worthy of our attention presents themselves."

"Very well," Watson said. "But I have a feeling we won't have to wait long. You know as well as I do that trouble has a way of finding us, whether we seek it out or not."

Chapter 2

As the afternoon wore on, the oppressive heat of the day seemed to seep into every corner of 221B Baker Street. Holmes had remained true to his word, barely moving from his chair save for the occasional stretch or shift in position. Watson, for his part, had busied himself with his journal, though he found his attention wandering more often than not, his gaze drawn to the window and the bustling street beyond.

The sudden, sharp rap at the door below startled both men from their respective reveries.

"I do hope," Holmes muttered, "that this isn't another distraught pet owner seeking our assistance."

Watson chuckled at his friend's dour expression. He rose from his chair and said, "I'll see to it this time, shall I?"

Without waiting for a response, Watson made his way down the stairs. As he reached for the door handle, he hoped that whoever stood on the other side might present a case worthy of Holmes' talents.

Upon opening the door, Watson was greeted by the sight of a well-dressed woman of mature years. Her attire spoke of wealth and refinement, from the cut of her fashionable dress to the gleam of her pearl necklace. Despite her obvious social standing, there was an air of distress about her, evident in the tight set of her jaw and the worried furrow of her brow.

"Good afternoon, madam," Watson said, offering a polite bow. "How may I be of assistance?"

The woman clasped her hands together. "Good afternoon. I'm here to see Mr Holmes. It's a matter of utmost urgency."

Watson replied, "Of course. Please, do come in. Mr Holmes is upstairs."

He led the woman upstairs and into the sitting room.

Holmes was on his feet, his earlier lethargy seemingly forgotten as he regarded their visitor with keen interest. He greeted the woman and invited her to take a seat.

The woman sank into the offered chair and said her name was Mrs Winthrop. "Mr Holmes, I've come to you because I'm in desperate need of your expertise. A valuable item has been stolen from my home. A Fabergé egg of considerable worth and sentimental value."

Holmes took a seat, Watson following suit. At Holmes' insistence, Mrs Winthrop gave more details of the theft.

"The egg in question was a gift from my late father. The deep blue enamel exterior is adorned with gold filigree and studded with diamonds. When opened, it reveals a miniature golden carriage inside. I keep it in a locked display cabinet in the family drawing room. Yesterday afternoon, I went to show it to a friend, and it was simply gone. It was most definitely there the day before that."

Holmes asked, "You reported this to the police, I take it?"

Mrs Winthrop's expression soured. "I did, but they were less than helpful. I reported it yesterday, and they visited my home this morning. But because there were no signs of a forced entry, they suggested I had simply misplaced it or that one of my staff might have moved it."

"But you disagree," Holmes prompted.

"Vehemently," Mrs Winthrop replied, her voice firm. "I know every inch of my home, Mr Holmes, and my staff are all trusted employees. This egg has been stolen, I'm sure of it."

Holmes got to his feet. "Mrs Winthrop, if it's convenient, Dr Watson and I shall visit your home immediately to investigate."

Relief washed over Mrs Winthrop's face. "Oh, thank you, Mr Holmes. I can't tell you how grateful I am. Yes, it is convenient for you to visit now. I shall go with you."

As Holmes bustled about the room, gathering his coat and various implements he deemed necessary for the investigation, Watson asked Mrs Winthrop for her address.

Mrs Winthrop provided her address, and Watson's eyebrows rose slightly at the mention of such a prestigious location.

Within minutes, the three of them were descending the stairs of 221B Baker Street. They stepped out onto the pavement and Holmes hailed a passing hansom cab with a sharp whistle.

They climbed aboard. Watson called out the address to the driver.

As the cab clattered over the cobblestones, Watson studied Mrs Winthrop's worried face. She sat rigidly, her hands clasped tightly in her lap, her gaze fixed on the passing streets.

"Mrs Winthrop," Watson said gently, "might I ask if there's any particular reason why someone would target this specific item? Beyond its obvious monetary value, of course."

"I'm not sure, Dr Watson. It's valuable, yes, but we have other items of worth in the house. Why this particular egg was taken, I couldn't say."

Chapter 3

A short while later, the hansom cab clattered to a halt outside the Winthrop residence. The imposing Georgian townhouse stood proudly amongst its equally impressive neighbours, its pale stone façade gleaming in the afternoon sun. Wrought-iron railings guarded a small but immaculately manicured front garden, where colourful blooms nodded in the gentle breeze.

Mrs Winthrop alighted from the cab first. Holmes followed, taking in every detail of their surroundings. Watson brought up the rear, fishing in his pocket for coins to pay the driver.

"This way, gentlemen," Mrs Winthrop said, leading them up the short flight of steps to the glossy black front door. But before she could open it, the door swung open.

A tall, thin man in his fifties stood in the doorway, impeccably dressed in the sombre attire of a butler. His face was a mask of professional neutrality, but Watson noticed a flicker of something in his eyes. Unease, perhaps?

"Ah, Simmons," Mrs Winthrop said. "This is Mr Holmes and Dr Watson. They're here to investigate the incident that I mentioned to you yesterday, and wish to see where it took place."

Simmons bowed slightly. "Very good, madam. Shall I show them to the family drawing room?"

"No need, Simmons. I'll take them myself."

"Of course, madam."

Watson caught Holmes' eye. The detective's slight nod confirmed that he, too, had noticed something off about the butler's demeanour.

The interior of the house was just as impressive as its exterior. They passed through a marble-floored entrance hall adorned with priceless artworks and Persian rugs, then went up a sweeping staircase to the first floor.

The family drawing room was a large, airy space, its tall windows looking out over the square. Elegant furniture in the Regency style was arranged around a magnificent fireplace.

Mrs Winthrop led them to a corner of the room where an ornate display case stood. Made of rich mahogany and glass, it contained a variety of small, clearly valuable objects: delicate porcelain figurines, exquisitely crafted snuff boxes, and several pieces of jewellery that glittered in the light of the room.

"The egg was here," Mrs Winthrop said, pointing to an empty velvet-lined space on the middle shelf. "This cabinet is always kept locked, and the key is placed in a safe in my husband's bedroom."

Holmes stepped closer and examined the case. Without a word, he reached into his pocket and withdrew a small tool. Before Mrs Winthrop could protest, he had inserted it into the lock and, with a deft twist, opened the case.

"Good heavens!" Mrs Winthrop exclaimed, her hand flying to her throat. "How did you do that? It shouldn't be that easy to open!"

Holmes turned to her. "I'm afraid, Mrs Winthrop, that this lock is of inferior quality. Any determined thief with even rudimentary skills could have opened it in seconds."

The colour drained from Mrs Winthrop's face. "It was sold to us as top-of-the-line. The most secure available."

"You were misled," Holmes said gently. "Now, tell me more about the egg itself. When did you last see it?"

Mrs Winthrop sank into a nearby chair, visibly shaken. "It was two days ago, in the afternoon. I had taken it out to show to my sister, who was visiting. We admired it for a while, then I put it back and locked the case. I checked the case to make sure it was locked. I then returned the key to the safe."

"And you're certain you replaced the egg in the case?" Holmes asked.

"Absolutely certain," Mrs Winthrop insisted. "I remember distinctly because my sister commented on how carefully I handled it. I always do, and not solely because of its monetary value. It was one of the last things my father gave me before he passed."

Holmes nodded sympathetically. "I understand. Now, Mrs Winthrop, if you wouldn't mind, I'd like to speak with your butler. Privately, if possible."

Mrs Winthrop looked surprised, but nodded. "Of course, Mr Holmes. I'll send Simmons in. Please, take as long as you need."

As Mrs Winthrop left the room, Holmes turned to Watson and asked, "What do you make of it so far?"

Before Watson could reply, there was a discreet knock at the door, and Simmons entered.

"You wished to see me, sir?" he asked, addressing Holmes.

"Yes. Please, come in and close the door."

The butler complied, standing stiffly before them, his hands clasped behind his back.

Holmes asked, "Simmons, how long have you been in Mrs Winthrop's employ?"

"Fifteen years, sir," Simmons replied promptly.

"And in that time, have you ever known anything to go missing from the house? Or misplaced?"

"No, sir. Never."

Holmes raised an eyebrow. "Come now, Simmons. Surely in fifteen years, something must have been misplaced at some point?"

The butler's jaw tightened almost imperceptibly. "I run a tight ship, Mr Holmes. Things do not go missing in this household."

Holmes nodded. "I see. I'd like to know more about the other staff members. This is a delicate question, but one I need to ask. Has anyone been experiencing financial difficulties recently?"

The butler shifted his weight almost imperceptibly. "I'm not sure that's relevant, Mr Holmes. The staff here are all of an impeccable character."

Holmes said, "I appreciate that, but even the most upstanding individuals can fall on hard times. It's not a reflection on their character to struggle financially."

Simmons hesitated, his attention darting briefly to Watson before returning to Holmes. "I don't feel comfortable discussing the private affairs of others, sir."

"I understand your reluctance," Holmes said, his tone softening slightly. "But I must remind you that a valuable item has been stolen. Any information could be crucial to recovering it."

The butler let out a small sigh. "Very well, sir. There is one member of staff who has been having some difficulties. It's Mrs Brimble, the cook. She's been with us for nearly a decade, and she's an excellent cook, truly. But..." He paused, looking uncomfortable.

"But?" Holmes prompted.

"She has a gambling problem," Simmons said. "I've tried to help her; to counsel her, but nothing has helped, and her debts have been mounting."

Watson interjected, "That must be a terrible burden for her to bear."

Simmons nodded. "She's a good woman at heart, just trapped in a vicious cycle. I can say for certain that Mrs Brimble is not a thief. She's been loyal to this household for years. I'd stake my reputation on her innocence."

Holmes said, "Your loyalty to Mrs Brimble is admirable, Simmons. However, we must explore every possibility.

Would it be possible for us to speak with Mrs Brimble in private?"

The butler looked uncertain, but after a moment, he nodded reluctantly. "Very well, sir. I'll fetch her for you. But please, I beg you to be gentle. Mrs Brimble is not accustomed to being questioned."

The butler left the room, closing the door behind him with a soft click.

Chapter 4

Mrs Brimble entered the drawing room a few minutes later, her hands twisting nervously in her apron. Her face was flushed and wisps of grey hair escaped from beneath her cap.

"Mrs Brimble," Holmes said gently, gesturing to a nearby chair. "Please, have a seat. We just have a few questions for you."

The cook hesitated, then perched on the edge of the chair, her back ramrod straight. "I've done nothing wrong," she blurted out. "I swear it."

Watson said gently, "We're not here to accuse you of anything, Mrs Brimble. We're simply trying to gather information about the missing Fabergé egg. Do you know anything about it?"

Mrs Brimble's eyes widened, and she clasped her hands tightly in her lap. "The egg? Oh, yes, I heard about that. Such a shame, it was. Beautiful thing, it was." She paused, then added hastily, "But I didn't take it! I would never betray Mrs Winthrop's trust like that. Never!"

Holmes observed her carefully, noting the beads of sweat forming on her brow. "Mrs Brimble, we understand you've been experiencing some financial difficulties lately. Is that correct?"

The cook's face crumpled, and tears welled up in her eyes. "I've been such a fool. The gambling just got away from me. But I swear, I've stopped now. I'll pay off every penny I owe, even if it takes the rest of my life."

Watson offered her his handkerchief and said softly, "What a terrible position for you to be in."

Mrs Brimble dabbed at her eyes. "It is. But I'm determined to make it right. I don't want my problems to affect my job. I couldn't bear to lose my position here. The Winthrops have been so good to me."

Holmes asked, "Mrs Brimble, can you think of anyone who might have taken the egg? Has there been any unusual behaviour among the staff recently?"

The cook shook her head vigorously. "No, sir. We're all loyal here. Everyone loves working for the Winthrops. I can't imagine any of us doing such a thing."

As Mrs Brimble spoke, the door to the drawing room burst open with a bang. A tall man strode in, his face flushed with anger.

The cook leapt to her feet. "Oh! Mr Winthrop! We weren't expecting you back so soon."

"Obviously," he replied in an icy tone. He glowered at Holmes and Watson. "What in blazes is going on here? Why is my cook crying? Who are you men, and what are you doing in my house?"

Holmes rose smoothly to his feet, extending his hand. "I'm Mr Holmes, and this is my colleague, Dr Watson. We were engaged by your wife to investigate the matter of the missing Fabergé egg."

Winthrop ignored Holmes's outstretched hand, his scowl deepening. "My wife did what? This is preposterous! The police are already dealing with this matter."

"With all due respect, Mr Winthrop," Watson interjected, also rising to his feet, "the police seemed to have dismissed the case rather quickly. Your wife was concerned and sought our expertise."

Winthrop's face reddened further. "Nonsense! The police know what they're doing. We don't need amateur detectives poking their noses where they don't belong."

Holmes raised an eyebrow at the man's vehemence. "I assure you, sir, we are far from amateurs. We've had considerable success in solving cases that have baffled the police."

"I don't care if you've solved every mystery from here to Timbuktu," Winthrop snapped. "This is my house, and I want you out of it. Now!"

Mrs Brimble, who had been watching the exchange with wide, fearful eyes, said, "Mr Winthrop, sir, please don't be angry. These gentlemen were just asking me some questions. They've been very kind."

Winthrop's gaze expression softened slightly. "It's all right, Mrs Brimble. You can go back to your duties now. I'll handle this."

Mrs Brimble scurried out of the room, casting one last anxious glance over her shoulder.

Winthrop turned back to Holmes and Watson. "I appreciate that you were trying to help, as was my wife when she hired you, I suppose, but your services are not required. The police are more than capable of handling this matter."

Holmes noticed the slight twitch in Mr Winthrop's left eye and the way his hands clenched and unclenched at his sides. "Very well, Mr Winthrop. We'll take our leave. But if you change your mind, you know where to find us."

Holmes and Watson swiftly left the house and walked away.

Holmes said, "Isn't it curious how Mr Winthrop seemed rather eager to get rid of us?"

Watson nodded slowly. "He did seem unusually agitated. Do you think he might be hiding something?"

"It's certainly possible. In fact, I'm beginning to wonder if Mr Winthrop himself might be behind the disappearance of the Fabergé egg."

"Mr Winthrop?" Watson asked. "But why would he steal from his own home?"

"Think about it," Holmes said. "What if Mr Winthrop is the one with financial problems? I don't know what his occupation is, but I suspect he holds a position of great authority. And if that is the case, he would go to great lengths to avoid any hint of financial instability. Perhaps he has pawned the item, or sold it to a discreet third party. He may have taken the necessary steps needed to bring in much-needed money."

Watson said, "Good Lord, Holmes. You might be onto something there. But how can we prove it?"

Holmes smiled. "Alas, now that we've been dismissed by Mr Winthrop, we are not in a position to prove anything. And yet, I have a feeling that we will be called back to this residence soon."

Chapter 5

Holmes and Watson approached 221B Baker Street, the summer heat still hanging heavily in the air.

Upon entering their lodgings, they were greeted by Mrs Hudson, their landlady, who emerged from the kitchen, a look of mild exasperation on her face.

"Oh, Mr Holmes, Dr Watson, I'm so relieved that you're back. There's a gentleman waiting for you in the sitting room. He's been here for nearly an hour, and I daresay he's growing rather impatient."

Holmes asked, "And who might this gentleman be, Mrs Hudson?"

"He says his name is Mr Carrington. A businessman of some sort, I believe. Seemed quite agitated, I thought."

Watson glanced at Holmes, noting the spark of interest in his friend's eyes. "Well, it seems our day is far from over, Holmes."

"So it would appear," Holmes replied. "Let us not keep Mr Carrington waiting any longer."

They entered the sitting room to find a well-dressed man pacing back and forth, his hands clasped behind his back. He was of medium height, with greying hair and a moustache. Upon seeing Holmes and Watson, he stopped abruptly.

"Mr Holmes, Dr Watson, thank goodness you've returned," he said. "I am Theodore Carrington, and I find myself in dire need of your assistance."

Holmes gestured for their visitor to take a seat, while he and Watson settled into their usual chairs. "Mr Carrington, tell us what brings you here."

Carrington settled into the offered chair. "It's a most distressing matter, Mr Holmes. A valuable item has been stolen from my home. A diamond tie pin that has been in my family for generations. It's extremely valuable. The diamond is a perfect blue, nearly three carats in weight, and set in platinum. It's not just the monetary value, you understand, but the sentimental importance to my family."

Holmes asked, "And where exactly was this tie pin when it vanished?"

"In my dressing room," Carrington replied. "I keep it in a small velvet box on my dressing table. I last saw it two nights ago. But when I went to retrieve it this morning, the box was empty and my tie pin gone."

"Were there any signs of forced entry to your residence?" Holmes inquired.

Carrington shook his head. "None whatsoever. That's what's so baffling about the whole affair. I've had the entire house searched from top to bottom, but with no luck. It's as if the tie pin simply vanished into thin air."

Watson said, "What about your staff, Mr Carrington? Do you have reason to suspect any of them?"

The man's face clouded. "I don't know what to think, Dr Watson. My staff has been with me for years. They're all loyal, trustworthy people. Or at least, I thought they were."

Holmes asked, "Mr Carrington, who else resides in your home? And who, besides yourself, would have access to your dressing room?"

"Well, there's my wife," Carrington began. "As for the staff, there's Mrs Perkins, our housekeeper, and her husband, who serves as our butler. Then there's the cook and two maids."

"And of these individuals, who would have a reason to enter your dressing room?" Holmes pressed.

Carrington shifted uncomfortably in his seat. "Well, Mrs Perkins oversees the cleaning of the entire house, including my dressing room. But Mr Holmes, I can't believe she would do such a thing!"

Holmes nodded thoughtfully. "I understand your reluctance to suspect those close to you, Mr Carrington. However, we need to explore every avenue. Now, tell me, have there been any unusual occurrences in your household recently? Any changes in routine or unexpected visitors?"

Carrington considered Holmes' question. "Not that I'm aware of. But I must confess, I'm often out on business matters or at my club. It's possible something unusual might have occurred, but has escaped my notice."

Holmes said, "I see. In that case, would it be possible for Dr Watson and myself to visit your home now? We'd like to speak with your staff and examine the scene of the theft."

Carrington hesitated for a moment, glancing at his pocket watch. "Yes, I suppose that would be acceptable. However, I must ask that you don't take too much time. I'm due at my club later today, and I don't want to be late."

"Of course," Holmes replied, rising from his chair. "We shall endeavour to be as swift and thorough as possible. Watson, if you're ready?"

Watson nodded. "Always, Holmes."

The three men made their way out downstairs and onto the street.

Carrington hailed a hansom cab, and they set off towards his residence. As they travelled, Holmes peppered their client with questions about his household, the layout of his home, and his daily routines.

Upon arriving at Carrington's impressive townhouse, which Holmes noticed wasn't far from Mrs Winthrop's home in Grosvenor Square, they were greeted at the door by a stern-faced woman in her fifties wearing a long black dress. Her grey hair pulled back into a tight bun.

"Mrs Perkins, I presume?" Holmes said, tipping his hat politely.

The housekeeper gave him a curt smile. "Yes, sir. And you must be Mr Holmes. We heard you might be coming."

Carrington stepped forward. "Mrs Perkins, Mr Holmes and Dr Watson are here to investigate the missing tie pin. Please ensure they have access to whatever they need."

Mrs Perkins nodded. "Of course, sir."

Carrington led Holmes and Watson up the grand staircase to his dressing room. The room was spacious and well-appointed, with large windows overlooking the back garden.

Holmes immediately set to work and examined the dressing table where the tie pin had been kept, running his fingers along the polished surface. He noted the empty, velvet box where the pie pin had been kept.

"Mr Carrington," Holmes said, not looking up from his examination, "do you keep your dressing room door locked?"

Carrington shook his head. "No, I'm afraid not. I've never felt the need, given the trust I place in my staff."

Holmes continued his examination.

Watson observed, taking notes in his book. He noticed Mr Carrington's growing impatience, the man repeatedly checking his pocket watch and shifting from foot to foot.

A few more minutes passed before Holmes said, "I've seen all I need to here. Can we speak with your staff now, Mr Carrington? I'd like to start with Mrs Perkins."

Carrington answered, "Yes, of course. Let me take you into the drawing room."

When they reached the drawing room, Holmes turned to Carrington and said, "I understand you're pressed for time. Perhaps Dr Watson and I could continue our inquiries with your staff while you prepare for your engagement?"

Carrington hesitated, clearly torn between his desire to be present for the investigation and his social obligations. "I suppose that would be acceptable, Mr Holmes. Mrs Perkins can show you out when you've finished. But please, do keep me informed of any developments. I'll have a word with Mrs Perkins now, and let her know you wish to see her."

"Thank you," Holmes said. "I assure you, we'll be in touch as soon as we have any news."

With that, Carrington excused himself, leaving Holmes and Watson to await the arrival of the housekeeper.

Chapter 6

A few minutes later, the door to the drawing room opened and Mrs Perkins entered, her face set in a mask of barely concealed hostility.

"Mrs Perkins," Holmes began, "thank you for joining us. We have a few questions about the missing tie pin. Please, take a seat."

Mrs Perkins immediately stiffened and remained standing. "I suppose Mr Carrington has accused me of theft, hasn't he? That man has never trusted me, not in all my years of service!"

Watson shifted uncomfortably, glancing at Holmes.

Holmes, however, remained unperturbed and said, "I assure you, Mr Carrington has made no such accusation. We're simply trying to gather information about the incident."

Mrs Perkins sniffed disbelievingly. "Well, I know nothing about it. I've been in this house for twenty years, and I've never so much as taken a penny that wasn't mine."

Holmes said, "I'm sure that's true, Mrs Perkins. Do you have any suspicions about who might have taken the item?"

At this, Mrs Perkins let out a harsh laugh. "Suspicions? I'll tell you this, Mr Holmes, anyone in this house could have done it. They're not all as trustworthy as I am, that's for certain." She began to pace, her agitation evident in every movement. "There's the maids, always gossiping and giggling. Who knows what they get up to when no one's looking? And the cook, always complaining about her wages. Then there's the gardener, skulking about at all hours."

Watson jotted down notes as Mrs Perkins continued her tirade. Holmes listened patiently.

"Mrs Perkins," Holmes interrupted gently, "what about your husband? I understand he's the butler here."

The housekeeper stopped her pacing abruptly, her face flushing. "My husband? There's no need to talk to him. I can vouch for his honesty myself."

"Nevertheless, we'd like to speak with him, if possible," Holmes insisted.

Mrs Perkins' mouth tightened into a thin line. She stood silent for a moment, her internal struggle visible on her face. Finally, she nodded curtly. "Very well. I'll fetch him for you. But I warn you, you're wasting your time."

As Mrs Perkins left the room, Watson said, "What do you make of her, Holmes?"

"She's certainly defensive. But whether that's due to guilt or simply a prickly nature remains to be seen."

The door opened once more. Mr Perkins entered, a thin, nervous man with fidgeting hands. He bowed slightly to Holmes and Watson, and asked how he might be of assistance.

Holmes gestured for Mr Perkins to take a seat. "Mr Perkins, we're investigating the disappearance of Mr Carrington's tie pin. We were hoping you might be able to shed some light on the matter."

Mr Perkins replied, "I'm afraid I don't know anything about it, sir. I've been attending to my duties as usual."

"I see," Holmes replied, his gaze intensifying. "The tie pin is of great value. Do you know anyone who might want to take it? Perhaps someone who is experiencing financial difficulties?"

The butler seemed to wilt under Holmes' focused attention. His hands twisted in his lap, beads of perspiration appearing on his forehead. Suddenly, he seemed to deflate, his shoulders sagging.

"I haven't taken the tie pin, sir. I swear it," Mr Perkins said. "But there is something I need to tell you. I've got a feeling you'll find out anyway, so I might as well tell you now."

Holmes nodded encouragingly. "Go on, Mr Perkins. You can trust us with your confidence."

Mr Perkins said, "I'm the one who has financial difficulties. I have a gambling problem. I owe a lot of money to some unsavoury characters. It's more money than I can ever hope to repay on my wages. But I didn't steal the tie pin. I'd never do that, no matter how desperate I was."

"Does your wife know about this, Mr Perkins?" Holmes asked gently.

Mr Perkins shook his head vehemently. "No, sir. And she can never know. She'd kill me if she found out. We've worked so hard to build a respectable life here. If she knew I'd risked it all..." He stopped talking, his face was a picture of despair.

"Mr Perkins," Holmes said, "I appreciate your honesty. Rest assured, we will be discreet with this information. However, I must ask, have you noticed anything unusual in the house lately? Anything that might be related to the missing item?"

"No," Mr Perkins replied. "I'm not aware of anything unusual. And as for suspicions, I trust everyone in this house. They would never steal anything. I know them well. We're like a family, you see."

Watson's eyebrows rose slightly at the butler's words, recalling Mrs Perkins's earlier tirade against her fellow staff members.

"Is there anything else you can tell us, Mr Perkins? Anything at all that might be relevant?" Holmes pressed gently.

The butler hesitated for a moment, then shook his head once more. "No, sir. I've told you all I know."

Holmes nodded and got to his feet. "Very well, Mr Perkins. Thank you for your time."

As the butler shuffled towards the door, Holmes heard a slight movement outside. The door opened, revealing Mrs Perkins standing rigidly in the hallway, her stern gaze fixed on her husband. Mr Perkins studiously avoided her gaze and hastened past his wife.

Holmes called out, "Mrs Perkins, would you mind joining us again for a moment?"

The housekeeper sighed heavily before entering the room. "Yes, Mr Holmes? What more can I possibly tell you?"

"I was wondering if there might be anyone else in the household we could speak with," Holmes began, but before Mrs Perkins could answer, the door swung open once more.

Carrington strode into the room. "Gentlemen," he said, addressing Holmes and Watson, "I hope your investigation is progressing well?"

Holmes inclined his head. "We're making some headway, Mr Carrington. However, there are still a few more individuals we'd like to interview."

Carrington said, "Well, I regret I must ask you to continue your investigation tomorrow, or the day after. I don't wish to disrupt my staff or my day any further. I'm sure you understand."

Watson opened his mouth to protest, but Holmes laid a hand on his arm. "Of course, Mr Carrington. We'll take our leave and return another time in the near future."

As they left the room, Watson noticed the look of relief that flashed across Mrs Perkins' face. Carrington escorted them to the front door, his manner polite but firm.

Once outside, Holmes and Watson walked in silence for a few moments.

Holmes broke the silence. "There's a pattern emerging, Watson. Did you notice?"

"You mean the gambling problems? Both Mrs Brimble and Mr Perkins admitted to financial difficulties due to gambling."

"Yes, that's part of it," Holmes nodded. "But there's more. Did you observe how quickly we were shown the door, not just here but at the Winthrop residence as well? In both cases, it was the man of the house who abruptly ended our investigation."

"You're right, Holmes. Mr Winthrop was quite brusque in dismissing us, and now Mr Carrington has done the same, albeit more politely."

They walked in silence for a few more paces before Watson ventured, "Do you think it's possible that Mr Carrington himself is behind the missing tie pin? Just as you suspect Mr Winthrop could be behind the missing egg? What if it's all part of a fraudulent insurance claim plan? Mr Carrington could have hidden the tie pin himself and then reported it stolen to collect the insurance money. And the same could be said for Mr Winthrop."

Holmes said, "It's certainly a possibility worth considering, Watson. We mustn't discount any theory at this stage. However, we must be careful not to jump to conclusions without sufficient evidence. One thing I am certain of, is that there is a pattern to these thefts. Once we work out what that pattern is, we will catch our thief."

"Or thieves," Watson added.

Chapter 7

As the summer heat intensified over the next few days, Holmes and Watson found themselves inundated with a series of similar cases. The sweltering weather seemed to bring with it a rash of thefts, each one more perplexing than the last.

One client came to them with a missing brooch situation. She said it was a priceless cameo brooch that had been passed down through generations. The client advised there had been no signs of any forced entry to her home, and it was as if the brooch had simply vanished.

Another client reported the disappearance of a pair of diamond earrings that had been stored in a jewellery box in her bedroom. Again, there were no visible signs of forced entry via any door or window.

A third client told Holmes and Watson about a precious gold watch that had been taken from his dressing room. It was a watch he only wore for special occasions, and he had worn it to a ball the night before, and it was only the next afternoon when he returned home from work, that he noticed it was missing. Despite already suspecting what the client's answer might be, Holmes asked if there were any signs at all of a forced entry. The client said no, and that he had made a thorough check of the residence.

Not only were the thefts the same, but all the clients lived within a few streets of each other. Furthermore, the majority of items had been taken from upstairs rooms.

One by one, Holmes and Watson visited the homes of their clients, and after looking at the rooms where the thefts occurred, they talked to those members of staff who were available at the time of their visit.

A pattern emerged amongst the staff they questioned, and they discovered that several of the servants had financial difficulties, but not related to gambling issues this time. Each person Holmes and Watson questioned advised they were loyal to their employers and would never steal from them.

When Holmes and Watson walked away from the home of their latest client, Watson said, "I'm losing faith in my insurance fraud theory. Surely, everyone can't put in a claim at the same time? And with them all living so close to each other. The insurance company would soon become suspicious."

Holmes replied, "I wouldn't dismiss that idea just yet, Watson. These people must move in the same social circles, and as such, know each other. Maybe they have worked together to come up with an elaborate insurance scheme. And if their insurance companies become suspicious, they would confirm the items had definitely been stolen, and even Sherlock Holmes couldn't solve the thefts."

Watson exclaimed, "Good Heavens! Surely they wouldn't dare use your name to lend credibility to fraudulent claims?"

"One would hope not," Holmes replied grimly. "And yet..." He trailed off, shaking his head as if to clear it. "This infernal heat, Watson. I fear it may be affecting my judgment. Perhaps a cool bath and a good night's sleep will bring clarity to our thoughts."

As they trudged up the stairs to their rooms later on, both men felt the weight of the unsolved mysteries pressing down on them, as heavy and oppressive as the summer heat that enveloped the city.

Chapter 8

As the clock struck nine on the following morning, the temperature in London had already climbed to an unbearable degree. The air hung heavy and still, promising another day of stifling heat. Despite the oppressive weather, Holmes seemed to have shaken off the lethargy that had plagued him the previous day.

"Watson, my dear fellow," he called out, striding into the sitting room with renewed vigour, "I propose we take our deliberations outside. A change of scenery might be just what we need to think more clearly."

Watson looked up from his newspaper, wiping a bead of sweat from his brow. "Outside, Holmes? In this heat?"

"Precisely because of this heat," Holmes replied. "Come, let us find a shaded spot at a nearby café. I have a strong feeling we're overlooking something rather obvious, something that will soon come to us if we change our surroundings."

Intrigued by his friend's enthusiasm, Watson rose and donned his lightweight summer jacket. The two men descended the stairs and stepped out into the sweltering London streets.

They walked briskly, despite the heat, until they came upon a quaint café. Some of the outdoor tables were nestled beneath a large, leafy tree. The shade offered a modicum of relief from the relentless sun.

"This will do nicely," Holmes declared, pulling out a chair for Watson before seating himself.

A waiter approached, and Holmes ordered two tall glasses of iced lemonade. As they waited for their drinks, Watson pulled out his notebook and began to review his notes.

"Now then, Holmes," he began, "let's go over what we know. In each household, we've found staff members with financial difficulties. Mrs Brimble at the Winthrops', for instance, admitted to gambling debts."

Holmes nodded. "Yes, go on."

"Then there's the matter of the homeowners themselves," Watson continued. "Their behaviour was rather odd, wouldn't you say? Mr Winthrop almost threw us out, and Mr Carrington was in quite a hurry to see us leave."

"Indeed," Holmes murmured, his gaze fixed on the buildings across the street.

The waiter returned with their drinks, and both men took long, grateful sips of the cool lemonade. Holmes remained silent, his eyes still trained on the opposite side of the street.

Watson continued reading his notes aloud. He asked Holmes a question, and when his friend didn't answer, Watson looked up and saw a bemused expression on Holmes' face.

Watson said, "What's going on? Have I missed something? Did something happen?" He looked left and right along the street.

Holmes laughed. "We have been so blind. We saw everything that was to be seen at those houses we visited, but we missed the obvious! I feel like such a fool, and that isn't something that happens to me often."

Watson frowned. "I've missed something, haven't I? Was it something I mentioned in my notes?" He looked back at his book.

Holmes shook his head. "It wasn't in your notes, and yet, it has been affecting our investigations since the very beginning. Look at the buildings across the street, Watson. What do you see?"

Watson turned to look. "I see buildings and shops. Nothing out of the ordinary, there. And some of them, no, most of them, have their windows open because of the heat." He broke into a smile. "Ah! I see it now. Open windows!"

"Exactly!" Holmes exclaimed, slapping his hand on the table. "Open windows, Watson! Did you notice any open windows during our investigations?"

"I didn't," Watson replied. "Did you?"

Holmes smiled. "No, I didn't. They could have been open, or they could have been closed. And this is precisely why I feel such a fool. I should have picked up on this immediately. We've been so focused on the possibility of an inside job or a fraudulent claim that we've overlooked the most obvious explanation. We could be dealing with a cat burglar, Watson, one with the audacity to commit their crimes in broad daylight!"

Watson's eyes widened as the implications sank in. "But surely someone would have noticed a stranger scaling the walls of these homes?"

Holmes shook his head. "That's just it. Who could be in a position to enter an upstairs open window, after checking they weren't being observed, of course. Who do we see on rooftops every day without giving it a second thought?

A chimney sweep, for one. Covered in soot, agile, and accustomed to navigating the treacherous slopes of London's rooflines."

Watson nodded, beginning to see the logic in Holmes's reasoning. "Yes, I suppose that's true. And what about people in the roofing trade? They're often up there, repairing tiles and such."

Holmes added, "And let's not forget the window cleaners. They're a common sight. And what about a gardener or tree-trimmer? They might easily explain away their presence on a ladder near an open window."

"By Jove, Holmes. When you list them all like that, it seems there are quite a few professions that might provide cover for an opportunist thief."

Holmes said, "Our culprit need not actually be employed in any of these trades. A clever disguise would suffice to allay suspicion long enough to carry out the theft."

"So, what do you propose we do next, Holmes?"

Holmes answered, "We must retrace our steps, Watson. We need to revisit the scene of the first theft and speak to Mrs Winthrop's staff again. I haven't forgotten that her husband wishes for the police to deal with this matter, but once Mrs Winthrop knows about our new insight, I am certain she will let us into the house again."

"Back to the Winthrop residence, then?" Watson asked, already reaching for his hat. "Let's hope we don't meet Mr Winthrop again."

Chapter 9

Holmes and Watson made their way back to the Winthrop residence. The streets were quieter than usual, with many seeking refuge indoors from the sweltering temperatures.

Holmes gestured towards the houses they passed. "Look, Watson. Nearly every upper-storey window is open. It's a veritable invitation for our enterprising cat burglar. I'm surprised we haven't been approached by more clients about missing items."

"Perhaps some people are not aware anything has gone yet," Watson pointed out.

As they approached the Winthrop residence, they looked upwards at the same time and noticed the upper windows of the stately home were open.

Holmes muttered to himself, "I can't believe I didn't notice this before."

Watson said, "You mustn't blame yourself, my dear fellow. I didn't notice either. And don't forget what intense heat from the sun can do to a person's state of mind, especially when they're not used to it."

They rang the bell, and after a moment's wait, were shown into the drawing room by the butler, who looked even more ill at ease than during their previous visit. Mrs Winthrop entered shortly.

"Mr Holmes, Dr Watson," she greeted them. "I'm afraid this isn't the best time. My husband could return at any moment, and he was most displeased about your last visit. I tried to reason with him, but as much as I love him, he can be as stubborn as a mule sometimes."

Holmes inclined his head politely. "We won't be long, Mrs Winthrop. We've merely come to ask a few additional questions about the day your Fabergé egg went missing. Specifically, we're curious about any tradespeople who might have visited that day."

Mrs Winthrop said, "Tradespeople? I'm afraid I don't recall any such visitors that day. But then, I don't always keep track of such things. Let me summon one of the maids." She moved to the side of the room, pulled on a bell-rope, and then returned to her chair.

Seconds later, a young maid, no more than twenty years old, entered the room. Her eyes were wide with curiosity as she curtsied to the gentlemen.

"Mary," Mrs Winthrop said, "these gentlemen would like to know if we had any tradespeople visit on the day the Fabergé egg went missing. Do you recall anything?"

Mary replied, "I'm not sure, ma'am. What sort of tradespeople do you mean?"

Holmes answered for Mrs Winthrop, "Perhaps a chimney sweep, or a window cleaner? Someone like that."

As Holmes spoke, Mary's face grew increasingly anxious.

Holmes, ever observant, noticed her discomfort immediately. "Mrs Winthrop," he said smoothly, "might we have a moment alone with Mary? Sometimes staff find it easier to speak freely without their employers present."

Mrs Winthrop replied, "Of course, Mr Holmes. I'll be in the conservatory if you need me." She left the room, closing the door behind her.

As soon as Mrs Winthrop was gone, Mary's posture changed. Her shoulders slumped, and she looked on the verge of tears.

"Now, Mary," Holmes said kindly, "please don't be alarmed. We're simply trying to get to the bottom of this mystery. Can you tell us what's troubling you?"

Mary took a deep breath. "I didn't let any tradespeople in that day, sir. But," she hesitated a moment, "I did let someone else in."

Chapter 10

Holmes asked Mary to take a seat, and once she had, he encouraged her to explain who had entered the building on the day the Fabergé egg went missing.

"It was a hot day, just like today," Mary said. "I was alone in the kitchen, trying to keep cool, when I heard a knock at the back door. When I opened it, there was an old woman standing there. She looked so distressed, and her eyes were red from crying. She said she'd lost her cat and had seen him jump from the back roof onto our upper windowsill. The cat had then gone through an open window and was inside our house. The woman was beside herself with worry."

Watson asked, "And you believed her story?"

Mary nodded vigorously. "Oh yes, sir. She seemed so genuine. She said she lived nearby, and her cat, Sebastian, must have been confused by the heat and he ended up on our roof instead of hers. She said he didn't normally behave like that and she was really worried about him. She begged me to let her in so she could get him. I offered to find Sebastian for her, but she said he didn't like strangers and would most likely scratch me. She promised she wouldn't be long."

Holmes said, "So, you let her in?"

Mary's cheeks flushed with embarrassment. "I did. I know I shouldn't have, but she seemed so harmless, and I felt sorry for her. She reminded me of my grandmother."

Holmes asked, "Did you accompany her upstairs?"

"No, sir," Mary admitted. "I told her to be quick about it, as the family was expected back soon. I stayed in the kitchen, keeping an ear out for any trouble."

"And how long was she upstairs?" Holmes pressed.

Mary frowned, thinking hard. "Not long, sir. Perhaps five minutes at most. Then she came back down, carrying the cat in her arms. She thanked me profusely and left through the back door."

"Mary," Holmes said gently, "is it possible that this woman could have entered the family drawing room during her time upstairs?"

The maid's eyes widened in horror as the implication of Holmes's question sank in. "I suppose she could have. But surely she wouldn't have? She was just a frail old lady, not a thief. She wouldn't have stolen that egg, would she?"

Watson said, "Sometimes appearances can be deceiving. Did you notice anything unusual about her? Any details that struck you as odd?"

Mary shook her head. "No, sir. She looked like any other old woman you might see. Grey hair, wrinkles, a bit stooped. She was wearing a long dress, and a shawl as well, despite the heat. I thought that was odd." Mary sighed. "What have I done? I shouldn't have let her in, I really shouldn't. What will Mrs Winthrop say?"

Holmes stood up abruptly, startling both Mary and Watson. "You were fooled by a cunning thief, as were others, I've no doubt. I'm sure Mrs Winthrop will show you some sympathy. Thank you, Mary. You've been most helpful. We won't keep you any longer."

Mary curtsied and hurried from the room.

Watson turned to his friend, a huge smile on his face and a twinkle in his eyes.

Holmes held up a hand. "Don't speak, Watson. I already know what you're going to say. Yes, this elderly woman is most likely the one who knocked at our door a few days ago. Such was my ill temper at the time, that I'm afraid I didn't pay much attention to her. But now that I think back to that incident, I recall that her description matches Mary's account perfectly. The audacity of the woman! To knock on our very door. Though I now realise she didn't mention her cat jumping through one of our open windows, so it seems she wasn't out to steal from us."

Watson's smile widened as a thought struck him. "Perhaps she was playing a game of cat and mouse with us, knowing full well who we are. Knowing that she had undertaken some audacious thefts and was about to undertake more, she must have gained some peculiar satisfaction from calling at our door that day. It seems we've underestimated our quarry, Holmes. What do you suggest we do next?"

Holmes answered, "We shall question the other victims of these thefts. We must determine if the same woman with her lost cat made an appearance at any of their residences. I suspect we will find similar stories to the one Mary told us. This woman is clever, using the heat and open windows to her advantage, and playing on people's sympathies with her tale of a lost cat. She only steals a small item each time, one that could be easily concealed upon her person. And, may I note, she only takes items that are of high value, so she must be an experienced thief. I suspect the so-called lost cat is hidden within her shawl when she knocks on the doors of her unsuspecting victims. That would explain why she is wearing a shawl in this heat. And her shawl would be the perfect way to conceal any stolen items on her person. Come, Watson, let's continue with our enquiries before this woman steals from anyone else."

Despite the relentless heat of the day, Holmes and Watson proceeded with their investigation and returned to the homes of those clients who had reported a lost item recently.

After speaking to more members of staff at each residence, their suspicions were confirmed. Each home had been visited by an elderly woman looking for her cat. The woman was always wearing a long dress and a shawl, and was extremely upset about her beloved pet, Sebastian. She always came to the back door of the property and spoke to a maid or a cook, who were taken in by her desperate pleas, and thus, let the woman into the house. And, the woman has turned up when most of the residents of the properties were out.

Once they had completed their enquiries, Holmes and Watson returned to Baker Street where they crafted a plan to catch the conniving cat burglar.

When the plan was completed, Holmes leaned back in his chair and said, "Watson, we'll set out early in the morning and put everything in place." He glanced towards the cloudless blue sky outside. "The only thing that will spoil our plan would be a change of weather. If it rains tomorrow, then I fear we will lose our chance to catch this woman."

Chapter 11

The next day dawned bright and clear, but as Holmes gazed out of the window at Baker Street, he noticed a few wispy clouds on the horizon. His keen eye for detail and understanding of meteorology led him to suspect that rain might be on its way. Nevertheless, he and Watson set out to implement their carefully crafted plan.

They began by visiting the houses on the streets where the previous thefts had occurred. At each residence, they warned the occupants about the cunning cat burglar and advised them to keep their windows closed, despite the heat. The residents, already on edge from the recent spate of thefts, were grateful for the advice and promised to heed it.

Their final stop was at a house that had not yet been targeted. The owner, a kindly woman named Mrs Fairclough, greeted them warmly at the door. Her eyes lit up with recognition at the sight of the famous detective and his companion. With great delight, she ushered them into her sitting room.

"Mr Holmes, Dr Watson, what an honour to have you in my home!" Mrs Fairclough exclaimed. "I've read all about your cases in the newspapers."

Holmes smiled politely, but quickly got down to business. He explained about the cat burglar and how Mrs Fairclough could help them set a trap. The plan was simple but risky: leave all the windows open and then vacate the house, leaving only a couple of staff behind, who would need to be advised of his plan.

Mrs Fairclough listened intently, her expression growing more serious with each word.

When Holmes finished, she nodded firmly. "Of course, I'll help. Anything to catch this dreadful thief and protect our neighbourhood."

With Mrs Fairclough's enthusiastic agreement secured, Holmes contacted the police. After some persuasion, they agreed to send a couple of officers to assist in the operation.

As the morning wore on, the plan was set in motion. Watson and the two police officers took up their hiding position in the house opposite Mrs Fairclough's, thanks to another kind neighbour who was eager to see the burglar caught. From their vantage point, they had a clear view of the front of Mrs Fairclough's residence.

Meanwhile, Holmes donned the guise of a window cleaner. He procured a ladder, bucket, and cloth, and began to clean the windows of the houses on Mrs Fairclough's street, starting at the back. As he worked, he kept a watchful eye on the surrounding area, looking for any sign of the elderly woman.

The sun continued to shine, but Holmes noticed the clouds increasing in number and density. He frowned, hoping the impending rain wouldn't put off the thief and ruin their carefully laid plans. Despite the threat of inclement weather, he persisted in his disguise, methodically cleaning windows and discreetly observing the street.

Time seemed to crawl by at an agonising pace. Holmes found himself checking his pocket watch more frequently as time passed by. He began to wonder if their carefully laid plan had somehow been compromised. Perhaps the elderly woman had caught wind of their trap and decided to lie low for the day.

Just as doubt began to creep into his mind, Holmes spotted a figure at the far end of the street. An elderly woman in a long dress and shawl was making her way along the back street, her gait slow but purposeful. As she drew nearer, Holmes' sharp eyes noticed the way her attention went from house to house, assessing each one with a calculating gaze that belied her frail appearance.

Holmes pretended to focus on his work, but he kept the woman in his peripheral vision. As she approached Mrs Fairclough's house, he saw a flash of movement beneath her shawl. A small, black paw popped out momentarily before being quickly tucked away. Holmes felt a surge of satisfaction. This was definitely their burglar, complete with her four-legged accomplice.

The elderly woman paused in front of Mrs Fairclough's home, her eyes widening as she took in the open windows. A smile of satisfaction appeared on her wrinkled face, but was quickly replaced by a look of distress. She pulled her shawl tighter around herself, obscuring the hidden cat from view, and approached the back door with faltering steps.

As she reached the door, Holmes watched in fascination as the woman's entire demeanour changed. Her shoulders slumped, her hands began to tremble, and tears welled up in her eyes. It was a masterful performance, one that would have fooled even the most discerning observer. Holmes found himself impressed despite the circumstances.

The back door opened, revealing one of Mrs Fairclough's maids, one who had been briefed on the plan. The elderly woman began to speak, her voice breaking with emotion as she relayed the tale of her missing cat, and how she had seen him go inside one of the open windows above her.

The maid played her part perfectly; her face a picture of sympathy. She opened the door wider and invited the woman in to search for her cat.

As the door closed behind them, Holmes allowed himself a small smile of triumph. He climbed down the ladder. The trap had been sprung; now it was time to catch their clever thief.

Chapter 12

Holmes raced around the corner and towards the house where Watson and the police officers were waiting. As he reached the window, he caught sight of his friend's anxious face peering out. With a series of quick, precise gestures, Holmes indicated that the elderly woman was inside Mrs Fairclough's residence.

Watson's eyes widened in understanding, and he turned to relay the message to the officers. In a flurry of movement, the door burst open, and Watson emerged, followed closely by two constables. They rushed towards Holmes, who was already moving towards the rear of Mrs Fairclough's house.

"Quietly now," Holmes whispered as they positioned themselves near the back door. "We mustn't startle her before she emerges."

The small group waited, and the minutes ticked by.

Suddenly, the door swung open, revealing the elderly woman. She cradled a sleek black cat in her arms, a triumphant smile playing across her weathered features. As her gaze fell upon the assembled group, her expression froze, the smile dying on her lips.

"We meet again," Holmes said smoothly. "I see you've found your cat."

The woman's arms tightened instinctively around the feline, which mewed in protest. She looked from face to face, assessing her situation with remarkable composure for one so suddenly cornered.

Holmes continued, "We believe you have stolen something from this property."

"I've done no such thing," the woman retorted. "I came here looking for my cat, nothing more."

"Perhaps a search would clarify matters," Holmes suggested, nodding to the constables.

As the officers approached, the woman's demeanour changed. She seemed to shrink into herself, as if trying to become invisible. The cat, sensing her distress, wriggled free and leapt to the ground, darting off into the garden.

The search of the woman was swift and thorough. Within moments, one of the constables pulled a glittering object from a cleverly concealed pocket in the woman's shawl. He held it up for all to see. It was a diamond bracelet.

"That's Mrs Fairclough's!" exclaimed the maid, who had appeared in the doorway. "It was in her bedroom this morning!"

Holmes focused his attention on the elderly woman and said, "I believe you are responsible for other thefts as well. Ones that have taken place on surrounding streets."

The woman's face contorted, a battle of emotions playing out across her features. For a moment, it seemed she might continue to protest her innocence. But then, as if a great weight had settled upon her, she sighed deeply and nodded.

"Oaky," she admitted. "Yes, I might have helped myself to some trinkets recently."

"But why?" Watson asked, speaking for the first time since their confrontation began.

The woman's eyes flashed with a sudden fire. "Why?" she repeated, her voice gaining strength. "Because they made it so easy! All those open windows, valuables left in plain sight. It was too good an opportunity to miss."

Watson shook his head in disgust.

The woman turned to Holmes. "And you, Mr Holmes. We've met before, you know. Several times, in fact. Though I doubt you recognise me at the moment."

She straightened her posture; the years melting away from her frame. No longer stooped, she stood tall and proud, her eyes gleaming with a mischievous light. She reached up and grasped her shawl, pulling it away with a flourish. The constables, who had been moving to restrain her, paused in confusion. Her hands moved to her head, grasping at her grey hair. With a quick tug, the wig came away, revealing a head of auburn hair neatly pinned up.

"Good Lord," one of the constables muttered, his eyes wide with disbelief.

The woman smirked, clearly enjoying their shock. She produced a handkerchief from her sleeve and began wiping at her face. The wrinkles that had marked her as elderly disappeared under her ministrations, revealing smooth skin and sharp features.

Holmes' eyes narrowed as recognition dawned. "Miss Millie Marbeck," he said. "I should have known."

Millie Marbeck, no longer the frail old woman but a striking figure in her early forties, offered a mocking curtsy. "Mr Holmes, always a pleasure. I was wondering how long it would take you to see through my little masquerade."

Watson looked between Holmes and the woman. "Holmes, you know this lady?"

"I do, Watson," Holmes replied. "Miss Marbeck is quite the accomplished thief. We crossed paths several years ago, before I met you."

Miss Marbeck's smile widened. "What fun we had, Mr Holmes. Especially with that last theft."

Holmes said, "Stealing from a grieving widow isn't what I would call fun, Miss Marbeck. But that particular episode ended with your arrest and a ten-year sentence, as I recall."

The woman laughed. "Did you really think a mere prison sentence would keep me confined for long? I have friends in high places, Mr Holmes. Friends who found my skills useful. It wasn't difficult to arrange for an early release."

Holmes asked, "Why did you call at my lodgings recently? Were you going to attempt a theft?"

Miss Marbeck replied, "I was tempted to do so, but no, it was merely to make contact and see if you recognised me. Which you didn't. Mr Holmes, you must be more observant, you really should." She turned to face the constables, holding out her wrists. "Well, gentlemen? Shall we get on with it? I'm sure you're eager to escort me to the nearest police station."

As one of the officers moved to handcuff her, the woman's eyes sparkled with amusement. "I shall say goodbye for now, Mr Holmes. I suspect we'll be seeing each other again sooner than you think."

Holmes raised an eyebrow. "I wouldn't count on it, Miss Marbeck. This time, I'll ensure your sentence is carried out to the full extent."

She laughed again as the handcuffs clicked into place. "Haven't you learned by now? I'm like a cat with nine lives. You may cage me for a time, but I'll always find a way to land on my feet."

As the constables led her away, she called over her shoulder, "Would you mind finding that cat and returning him to his rightful owner? I think she lives somewhere on the next street to you, Mr Holmes. Do give her my apologies for stealing him, well, borrowing him for a little while."

Watson muttered something under his breath, which quite surprised Holmes.

"Well," Watson said, justifying his curses. "Stealing items is one thing, but taking someone's beloved pet is another matter altogether. What a terrible woman. I hope we never see her again."

"Me too," Holmes said, "Me too, Watson. Now, let's find this cat and return him to his owner. The clouds are gathering and it's going to start raining soon."

Chapter 13

The rain began, and it continued solidly, which was a welcome relief to the people of London.

A few weeks after Miss Marbeck's arrest, Holmes was settled in his armchair, listening to the patter of rain against the windows of 221B Baker Street. Watson, seated at the writing desk, was sorting through a small pile of correspondence that Mrs Hudson had just delivered.

"I say, Holmes," Watson said, breaking the companionable silence that had settled between them. "We've received quite a few letters from our recent clients."

Holmes raised an eyebrow. "And what do they have to say for themselves?"

Watson cleared his throat and began to read from the topmost letter. "This one's from Mrs Winthrop. She writes, 'My dear Mr Holmes and Dr Watson, I cannot express my gratitude enough for your invaluable assistance in recovering my beloved Fabergé egg. The police have returned it to me, and I am overjoyed to have it back in my possession. Your remarkable skills and dedication to justice are truly a credit to our fair city.'"

Holmes smiled. "How very gracious of her. I trust the other letters are of a similar vein?"

"Oh, yes. Mr Carrington sends his heartfelt thanks for the return of his...what was it again? Ah, yes, his diamond tie pin." He quickly looked through the remaining letters. "All the other items have been returned, too. It gladdens my heart to know Miss Marbeck never got the opportunity to sell them. No doubt, her plan was to add more to her collection and then sell the lot to the highest bidder."

Holmes nodded, a distant look on his face.

Watson set the letters aside and regarded his friend with curiosity. "You seem rather pensive, Holmes. Is something troubling you about the case?"

"Not troubling as such," Holmes said. "I find myself rather impressed by Miss Marbeck's ingenuity."

"Impressed?" Watson echoed. "But Holmes, she's a criminal!"

"Indeed she is," Holmes agreed. "And a most accomplished one at that. Consider the elegance of her plan: disguising herself as a harmless old woman, taking advantage of the open windows during the heatwave, and targeting only a single item from each household. It was a masterful piece of misdirection."

Watson frowned, clearly uncomfortable with his friend's admiration for the criminal mind. "But surely you don't condone her actions?"

Holmes chuckled, shaking his head. "Of course not. But one can appreciate the artistry of a well-executed plan without approving of its ends. Miss Marbeck's scheme was clever, daring, and very nearly successful. It's a pity she has chosen to apply her considerable talents to unlawful pursuits."

"Well," Watson said with a wry smile, "I suppose it's fortunate for London that you have chosen to apply your talents to solving crimes rather than committing them. I daresay you'd make a formidable criminal yourself, Holmes. I doubt even Scotland Yard's finest would stand a chance of catching you."

Holmes laughed outright at this, his eyes twinkling with amusement. "My dear Watson, you flatter me. Though I must admit, the thought has crossed my mind on occasion. The challenge of crafting the perfect crime, of outwitting the authorities. It would be a most stimulating intellectual exercise."

"Holmes!" Watson exclaimed, half-scandalised and half-amused. "You're not serious, surely?"

"Relax, old friend," Holmes said, waving a dismissive hand. "It's merely an academic consideration. I much prefer being on the right side of the law. There's far more satisfaction in bringing criminals to justice than in evading it."

Watson relaxed, chuckling softly. "Well, I'm certainly glad to hear that. I would hate to think of having to visit you in prison."

"Your concern is touching, Watson," Holmes said dryly. "But I assure you, if I ever did decide to turn to a life of crime, I would be far too clever to allow myself to be caught and imprisoned."

Watson agreed wholeheartedly, and then returned to the letters of thanks from their clients.

The case of the cat burglar was closed, but for Holmes and Dr Watson, there would always be new mysteries to solve and new challenges to face.

A note from the author

For as long as I can remember, I have loved reading mystery books. It started with Enid Blyton's Famous Five, and The Secret Seven. As I got older, I progressed to Agatha Christie books, and of course, Sir Arthur Conan Doyle's Sherlock Holmes.

I love the characters of Sherlock Holmes and Dr Watson, and the Victorian era that the stories are set in. It seemed only natural that one day, I would write some of my own Sherlock stories. I love creating new mysteries for Mr Holmes, and his trusty companion, Dr John Watson. It's not just the era itself that seems to ignite ideas within me; it's also the characters who were around at that time, and the lives they led.

This story has been checked for errors, but if you see anything we have missed and you'd like to let us know about them, please email mabel@mabelswift.com

You can hear about my new releases by signing up to my newsletter: www.mabelswift.com   As a thank you for subscribing, I will send you a free short story: Sherlock Holmes and The Curious Clock.

If you'd like to contact me, you can get in touch via mabel@mabelswift.com I'd be delighted to hear from you.

Best wishes

Mabel

Printed in Great Britain
by Amazon